Avocado Baby

Persea gratissima

A Red Fox Book

Published by Random House Children's Books
20 Vauxhall Bridge Road, London SW1V 2SA

A division of Random House UK Ltd
London Melbourne Sydney Auckland
Johannesburg and agencies throughout the world

Text and illustrations © John Burningham 1982

1 3 5 7 9 10 8 6 4 2

First published in the United Kingdom
by Jonathan Cape 1982

First published in Mini Treasures edition
by Red Fox 1999

The right of John Burningham to be identified as the author of this work has been
asserted by him in accordance with the Copyright, Designs and Patents Act, 1988.

Printed in Singapore.

RANDOM HOUSE UK Limited Reg. No. 954009

ISBN 0 09 940002 2

Avocado
Baby

John Burningham

Mini Treasures

RED FOX

For Emma

Mr and Mrs Hargraves and their two children
were not very strong. Mrs Hargraves was
expecting another baby, and they all hoped
it would not be as weak as they were.

The new baby was born and all the family were very pleased. Mr and Mrs Hargraves brought the baby home and it grew but, as they feared, it did not grow strong. Mrs Hargraves found feeding the baby difficult. It did not like food or want to eat much.

"Whatever can I do," wailed Mrs Hargraves.
"The baby doesn't like eating anything I make
and it looks so weak."
"Why don't you give it that avocado pear?"
said the children.

In the fruit bowl on the table there was an avocado pear. Nobody knew how it had got there because the Hargraves never bought avocados. Mrs Hargraves cut the pear in half, mashed it and gave it to the baby, who ate it all up.
From that day on an amazing thing happened. The baby became very strong.

It was getting so strong it could

break out from
the straps on its
high chair,

pull other children uphill in a cart.

wrench off the side of its cot.
And each day Mrs Hargraves gave
the baby avocado pear.

One night a burglar got into the house.

The baby woke up and heard the burglar
moving about downstairs.
The baby picked up a broom,

and chased the burglar. The burglar was so
frightened at being chased by a baby that he
dropped his bag and ran out of the house.

The next day Mr Hargraves put a notice
on the gate. "That should keep the
burglars away," he said.

The baby would help
carry the shopping,
move the furniture
and push the car when
it would not start.

One day two bullies were waiting for
the children in the park.

The bullies started being very nasty to the children. The baby did not like that and jumped out of its push-chair,

picked up the bullies and

threw them into the pond.

The baby gets stronger every day and of course it is still eating avocado pears.

Persea gratissima